Mischievous Stories

© 2018 David M. Merritt

aka Dave Merritt

All rights reserved. In accordance with the U.S. Copyright Act of 1976, the scanning, uploading, and electronic sharing of any part of this book without the permission of the author constitutes unlawful piracy and theft of the author's intellectual property. If you would like to use material from the book (other than for review purposes), prior written permission must be obtained by contacting the author at dave.merritt@comcast.net.

Thank you for your support of the author's rights.

ISBN-13: 978-1719163644

ISBN-10: 1719163642

060007042019

While a depiction of real events and characters, this is a work of fiction and does not claim to be historically accurate.

Printed in the United States of America

Mischievous Stories

Table of Content

Acknowledgments – iii

Preface – iv

Dedication – v

Thanks – vi

Clippings & Photo – vii

Chapter One – The Arrow – 1

Chapter Two – Electricity – 19

Chapter Three – Snake Pond – 41

Chapter Four – Prowling – 51

Chapter Five – Alligators in South Georgia Prowling – 67

Chapter Six – That Darn Hammer – 81

Chapter Seven – Big Tires – 89

Afterword – 99

Acknowledgments

Mischievous Stories has benefitted greatly from the generosity and hard work of others: Linda Merritt for support and early content editing; to Nadya Sagner for professional editing services nearer to publication; to Colonel (Retired) Bill Jenks, my "battle-buddy" in Battalion Command and a great friend, for his edit to this book and to Ryan Merritt, my daughter-in-law who found yet a few more mistakes.

Also, to Christina Cartwright at digitelldesign.com for her story interpretations that resulted in accurate or humorous illustrations of each chapter.

To Mackenzie Merritt and Hunter Beach, both grandchildren, who provided the motivation for me to write this book and some "grade level" editorial and opinion services.

To my three other grandchildren – Charlotte Merritt, Casey Merritt and Noah Beach for loving me and being such great kids.

Lastly, and most importantly, to my wife Shelia for her gift of the time is took to write, structure, and publish this first book of short stories.

While the preponderance of stories in this book are somewhat mischievous in nature, not all are rooted in mischief and the final chapter, "Big Tires" introduces my intent to continue this short story series into adulthood and into the realm of military stories.

Preface

God provides the opportunity for mortals to chart their own course in life and, for the most part, leaves us alone to fail miserably or succeed excessively or something in between. Why we are here on this earth is yet to be revealed, but in one near-death experience after the other, one must ask, why in the world am I still alive?

For what purpose do I exist?

I do not spend hours on end thinking about this. In appropriate time, I believe that God will likely reveal to me why I existed, what I did well, and what did not go so well. I can only hope and pray that my shortfalls will be less noticeable and impactful than my strong points.

These stories are true, and I hope you enjoy each and every one.

Dedication

This book is dedicated to the most wonderful wife a person could have, Shelia Diann Tomey Merritt. Without her, little success in my life would have been possible. She encouraged me, critiqued me, supported me, and loved me throughout my adult life. She gave me two wonderful children who provided five splendid grandchildren. I am proud of all my family and of what they have become. And, I note with great pride, the grandchildren who gave me a reason to write this book and who love me unconditionally.

I also dedicate this book to my parents, John Wiley Merritt and Willie Gene Patten Merritt. They raised four boys in the heat of South Georgia, were of modest means, understood the value of hard work and family, and supported their children every step of the way from birth to adulthood. They were people of good character and they loved their children and each other with all their might.

Thanks

My life was heavily influenced by the United States Army for 27 years, and by corporate America for seventeen years before I settled down to a home office to write this first collection of stories. Unintentional soldier-mentors like Colonel Al Luster, Lieutenant General Joe Laposata, Brigadier General Buck Walters, Major General Ken Guest, Chief Warrant Officer John Lowes, Major General Jim Wright, Major General Tom Glisson, Mr. Dick Weis, and Sergeant Major Billy Smith supported, motivated, and developed my professional character and career while giving me leeway to chart the course ahead. On the corporate side, Mr. Brian Dickson, Colonel (Retired) Mike Maloney, Mr. Andrew Fairbanks, Ms. Luanne Pavco, and Mr. Adam Jelic were particularly noteworthy and served as great mentors and friends throughout my civilian career.

From Private to Lieutenant Colonel and for my seventeen years in corporate America, each of these leaders, in their own way, helped me succeed and for each of them as well as others not mentioned here, I am deeply grateful.

Mischievous Stories

Clippings and Photo

Below-left: Newspaper Article Courtesy of the Tifton Gazette
Below-right: Newspaper Article from The News Examiner

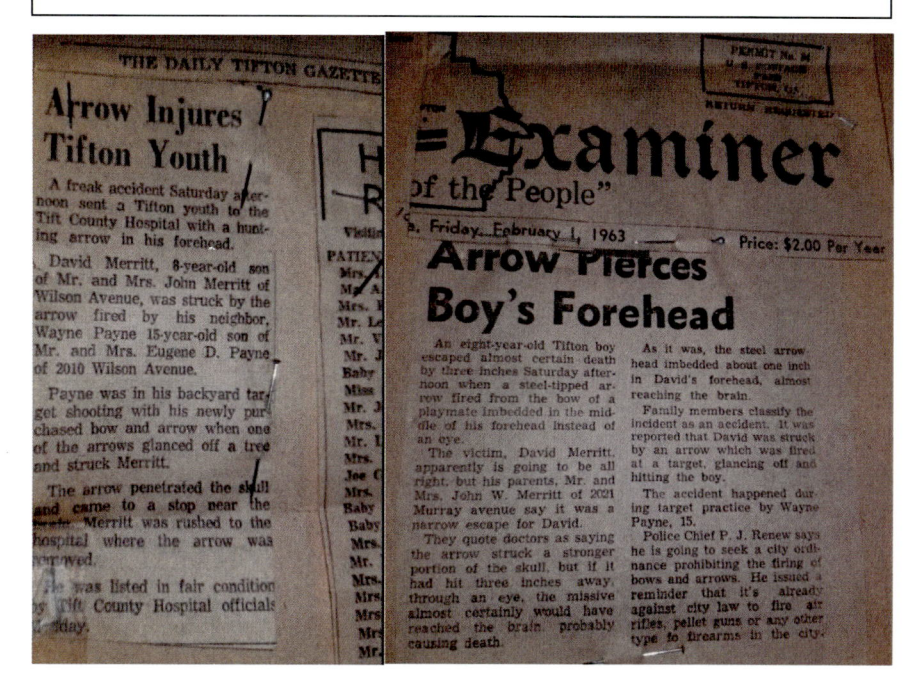

Arrow Injures Tifton Youth

A freak accident Saturday afternoon sent a Tifton youth to the Tift County Hospital with a hunting arrow in his forehead.

David Merritt, 8-year-old son of Mr. and Mrs. John Merritt of Wilson Avenue, was struck by the arrow fired by his neighbor, Wayne Payne 15-year-old son of Mr. and Mrs. Eugene D. Payne of 2010 Wilson Avenue.

Payne was in his backyard target shooting with his newly purchased bow and arrow when one of the arrows glanced off a tree and struck Merritt.

The arrow penetrated the skull and came to a stop near the *___*. Merritt was rushed to the hospital where the arrow was removed.

He was listed in fair condition by Tift County Hospital officials *___*day.

THE EXAMINER of the People

Friday, February 1, 1963 — Price: $2.00 Per Year

Arrow Pierces Boy's Forehead

An eight-year-old Tifton boy escaped almost certain death by three inches Saturday afternoon when a steel-tipped arrow fired from the bow of a playmate imbedded in the middle of his forehead instead of an eye.

The victim, David Merritt, apparently is going to be all right, but his parents, Mr. and Mrs. John W. Merritt of 2021 Murray avenue say it was a narrow escape for David.

They quote doctors as saying the arrow struck a stronger portion of the skull, but if it had hit three inches away, through an eye, the missile almost certainly would have reached the brain probably causing death.

As it was, the steel arrow head imbedded about one inch in David's forehead, almost reaching the brain.

Family members classify the incident as an accident. It was reported that David was struck by an arrow which was fired at a target, glancing off and hitting the boy.

The accident happened during target practice by Wayne Payne, 15.

Police Chief P. J. Renew says he is going to seek a city ordinance prohibiting the firing of bows and arrows. He issued a reminder that it's already against city law to fire air rifles, pellet guns or any other type of firearms in the city.

Figure 1: Photo of actual arrow…

Mischievous Stories

Chapter One – The Arrow

In small towns across America, and for that matter around the world, children often do not have a lot of things to do during their non-school time. If the children grow up on the farm, there are often chores to be done – feed the pigs, gather the eggs, clean out the barn, and other such tasks. But if you grow up in the city or in a small town and not on the farm, it is not always easy to find something to do. In places like that, children often make up games that keep them busy or they find ways to make money.

I was a normal child at the age of eight. I was full of energy, wore black glasses, and had very short hair that my father often cut on our back porch while we sat on a ladder. I had bad teeth, blue eyes, and a passion for having fun. I could run faster than anyone on my block, and since I was the smallest kid on my block, I always enjoyed a good foot race; sometimes those races kept me safe from harm by a bigger kid who might want to have some sort of confrontation. But those were very few and far between as the group of boys my age were all friendly and we all got along well. And, fortunately for me, I had a big brother who would, in a pinch, take up for me when it was necessary.

On Saturday, January 26, 1963, I found myself bored. I didn't have anything to do. No chores, no money-making job like cutting grass, and no friends to hang out with. So I left my yard in Tifton, Georgia, and headed down the tree covered alley towards 20th Street. The alley was dirt and there were trash cans on each side belonging to the people who lived in each home along the way.

I crossed the alley about halfway down the block and cut through a neighbor's backyard, passed the driveway, and into the front yard.

There, I saw four or five of my friends, all about my age, playing in the front yard of another neighbor's home. But they were not playing, they appeared to be hiding behind large pine trees. What were they doing? At first, I thought it was a game of hide and seek. Why did they crouch down behind these huge pine trees? The answer was soon to be provided and I would join them in this "business."

"We are fetching arrows for Wayne," explained one of my friends. "And for every arrow you collect, and run back to him, you get a penny."

The idea was that these four or five boys were in a yard and Wayne Payne, a sixteen-year-old boy, would use his brand-new fancy compound bow to shoot arrows into the air from his front yard, across another front yard, and into the third yard. Dale, Daryl, Allen, Tommy, and Terry already had strategic positions behind pine trees in the target area. When the arrow came down into the ground, the boy who could run to it and grab it first would run it back to Wayne and collect a penny for the returned arrow.

Now a penny does not sound like much money, but back in the 1960s, a penny was a lot of money. You could buy three pieces of candy for a penny at the convenience store on the corner of 20th Street and Highway 41. For a dime, you could buy a bottle of ice cold Coca-Cola. Just a few years earlier a nickel and a penny placed in the Coke machine would get you a fresh cold bottle. On a sizzling hot summer day, it was particularly good regardless of price.

"Can I play?" I asked.

"Sure," responded my friends. So I picked a tree in the middle of the yard and hid behind it. One of my buddies said, "You should not use that tree to hide behind. Most of the arrows come down there and you might get hit." "Good, I will make more money," I said as I took my place behind the large pine tree that was wider than my shoulders and waited for Wayne to shoot the first arrow.

As expected, and as the other boys had said, arrow after arrow came down near my spot in the yard. I was safe and sound behind my big pine tree and soon I had collected five or six arrows, ran them back to Wayne, and collected my reward. The other boys were making money too, but I was really in a good spot to make a lot of money fast!

At first Wayne was shooting arrows that had a metal tip that was round but not too sharp. You could touch the end of the arrow with your finger and it would not hurt you. But then, after a little while, he switched to deer hunting arrows with razor blades on four sides. They were sharp and quite pointed at the end of the arrow. If you touched the end of the arrow with your finger, it would cut you. Sharp indeed!

Sometimes the arrows Wayne would shoot got stuck in a tree. When that happened, we would stop the game, climb the tree, and get the arrow down. After that, everyone would go back to their spot and the "game" would continue.

I made it my habit to hide behind my tree, watch Wayne shoot the arrow, and then get my head behind the pine tree and wait for the arrow to come down around me. I would then run to the arrow, pull it from the ground, run it back to Wayne, and collect my penny.

Mischievous Stories

As Wayne prepared to shoot the next arrow, I watched him. When he drew the mighty bow back, pointed it into the air, and released the arrow, I quickly got behind my tree and waited. It seemed to take a long, long, long time for the arrow to come down. But I waited patiently and finally decided that perhaps the arrow had gotten stuck in a tree. When I concluded that the arrow must be stuck high in one of the trees, I poked my head out from behind the pine tree. When I did, everyone started getting up from behind their tree. And they started walking toward me. Why?

I looked all around as the other boys came my way. Was the arrow in the ground around me? Was it stuck in a tree near me? Did it come down behind me?

I looked around quickly to find the arrow but did not. Then I looked out in front of me, across one front yard and into Wayne's yard. When I saw Wayne, two front yards down the street, I realized why all the boys were coming my way. The arrow was sticking out of my head! This ultra-sharp razor blade deer-hunting arrow had sped through the air and struck me right in the center of my forehead. I could reach out and touch the end of the arrow that was stuck in my head.

Surprisingly, there was no blood and no pain. The impact of the arrow did not knock me down when it struck my head. I did not even know I had been hit.

As the other boys gathered around me, I saw Wayne throw down the bow he had been holding and run through his next-door neighbor's yard and into the yard where I stood. When he arrived, the other boys gathered around as Wayne tried to pull the arrow from my head.

To pull out the arrow, he first tried just tugging on it, but it would not come out. Then he put my head under his arm and reached across his chest with his other hand and tried to pull the arrow out. My head was in a vise created between his chest and his arm.

The arrow would not move.

"Can you wait a couple of hours before you tell anyone?" Wayne asked.

"No," I replied. "I better go home."

As I walked through the backyard where I was shot, then into and down the alley, the arrow stuck straight out of my head, pointing the way. When I walked through the bushes separating my yard from my next-door neighbor's yard, I encountered my brother Fred and my cousin Frank.

"Oh, that's neat," commented Fred. "Where did you get that?

He thought the arrow was one of those toys that appeared to be stuck in your head, but there was a wire that ran around the head to hold it in place.

"It's not a toy, it's real!" I exclaimed.

About that time our maid saw me. A very nice lady, she was pretty much in charge of raising me and my brother while our parents were at work. She had come outside to hang clothes on the line since we did not have a clothes dryer in our modest home.

When she saw me, she dropped the basket of clothes and ran into the house. I followed not too far behind her.

"Ms. Merritt, Ms. Merritt, your boy has been shot!" she shouted to my parents as she made her way down the hall to the bedroom where my parents were napping.

"Now, Essie May, that's not funny and we should not joke about such things," said my mother. About that time, I walked into the room. Both my parents levitated off the bed, or so it seemed. Anyway, up they sprang, ushering me down the hall and outside.

My father was a stout man, and a good man. He was honest, hardworking, and loved his family very much. However, he was no doctor. Except for the time he spent in World War II in Europe, he worked exclusively for Armour and Company. They prepared and sold meat products such as steak, turkey, and hot dogs to stores who then sold it to their customers. Once we got outside, he decided he would pull out the arrow. We tried it again in much the same way Wayne tried to pull it out. But to no avail. It would not come out. It was stuck!

"Get in the car," my father directed.

I sat in the back seat on the passenger side and my mother sat in the back seat beside me. We had to sit in the back seat because the arrow was so long, if I sat in the front seat, it would hit the windshield. Off we went to the hospital at record speed.

"Why are you laughing?" I asked my mother as we drove toward the hospital. "I'm not laughing, I am crying," she replied. I had never heard my mama cry and I didn't care for it too much. But it was a quick five-minute drive to the Tift County Hospital as my dad pushed the gas pedal to the floor.

"Get a doctor!" commanded my father as we came through the emergency room door.

"Which one?" asked the nurse, after she did a double take of me walking in the door with an arrow in my head.

"Any of them," my father replied.

In only a moment or two, Dr. Pitman, my pediatrician, walked around the corner and my dad said, "He'll do."

In a flash, Dr. Pitman ordered an x-ray of my head. I was walked into the x-ray room at this small hospital in Tifton, Georgia, and laid face up on a table. The x-ray was painless and only took a few moments. From there, it was back to the treatment area that looked much like an operating room – perhaps it was.

There, Dr. Bridges, another local pediatrician, joined Dr. Pitman and they began to work on me. The first step was to give me five shots in a circle around the arrow that stuck out of my forehead straight up into the air. I thought this would hurt a lot, but it didn't hurt at all. Really, no pain. After a moment, Dr. Bridges told me he was going to hold my head down on the table while Dr. Pitman pulled out the arrow. But guess what, Dr. Pitman could not pull it out.

He tried his best and yet it would not come out. Then he climbed onto the table and stood over me. One foot on each side of my head. He bent over, grabbed the arrow with both hands along the wooden shaft, and pulled while Dr. Bridges held down my head. It did not work. The arrow would not budge. And Dr. Pitman's hand slid from where he gripped the arrow near my head to the top of the arrow near the feathers. He could not hold it tight enough to pull it out.

"Let me get a pair of pliers," he said to Dr. Bridges. He then walked out into the waiting area and asked, "Does anyone have a pair of heavy-duty pliers?" My father had a set of heavy-duty electrical pliers in the trunk of his car, and he retrieved them.

The doctor came back into the operating room area. "Let's try this again," he said as he climbed up onto the table. He gripped the arrow with the pliers and pulled. The wooden part of the arrow came out. It seems that an arrow, in those days, was composed of three parts. The wooden part, a small round metal ring called an O-ring, and the arrowhead itself.

So, with the wooden part of the arrow pulled out, he focused his attention on the arrowhead, but instead he got only the O-ring. Then he tried again, and the arrowhead actually came out of my head.

There was no blood, except a drop or two, and no pain. Dr. Pitman gave me two stitches to seal the wound and sent me to a room in the hospital. There I remained for five days.

"Here is a dollar," my mother said as she left me some coins. There were vending machines in the hospital and she wanted me to have some money in case I wanted a beverage or snack. I think the cost of a Coke was about a dime at the time. Only a couple of years earlier, a Coke was only six cents.

My father brought in a cigar box and I put the coins in there for safekeeping and easy access. Our small-town hospital had never seen an accident of this type and it turns out that I would have to stay in the hospital for about a week before being sent home. During that time, an article would be published in the local newspaper, The Daily Tifton Gazette.

My mother spoke to others about the accident and reporters from a newspaper in Atlanta, Georgia, called her for an interview. She told them most of what happened and how I was getting along.

Interestingly, I became somewhat of a freak show. People would walk down the hospital halls, stick their head in my room, or just walk in to say hello to my mother and check on me. On my first day in the hospital, a kind lady entered the room to visit my mother and me. While she was there, I took out my cigar box and coins and began counting my pennies, nickels, dimes, and quarters that all together totaled only one dollar.

"My goodness," exclaimed the kind lady, "you have a small fortune there, young man."

"Yes ma'am," I responded. "Mama gave me some change, so I could buy a Coke if I got thirsty."

"Well, let me add a little bit to your cigar box bank," said the nice lady as she reached into her purse and extracted some change. "Wow!" I exclaimed and thanked her for the coins. As I recall, my bank account doubled at that very moment and I now had two dollars on my first day in the hospital after the arrow had been extracted from the center of my forehead.

And so it went, day after day for the five days I remained in the hospital. By the time my hospital stay was over, I had accumulated about $93.00 in hard cold cash. Now that might not sound like much today, but you must remember that a bottle of Coke was ten cents and candy was one cent for three Tootsie Tolls. So, $93.00 was a fortune!

Counting the money wasn't hard work, and the more I counted, the more I made. Life was good.

For my entire stay in the hospital, the nurses and doctors wanted me to lie flat on my back. They were scared what might happen if I stood up. So, lying on my back it was. No getting up, no walking, no exercises were the orders of the day from Saturday until Wednesday. But on Thursday, it was time to get up and walk.

When I got out of bed, I stood next to the bed for a grand total of four or five seconds before I fell to the floor. The nurse was holding onto me, but I still went down onto the cold tile floor. My legs had gotten so weak that I could not even stand on my own two feet. The nurse helped me back into bed and then had me do some exercises with my legs. Later that day, we tried it again with better results. First I walked to the end of the bed and back, then to the door and back, and finally into the hallway and around the hospital a bit. All was well, and my brain did not fall out of the hole that was in my head and stitched closed.

About 50 years later, I had to have an x-ray of my head. Guess what? The hole in my skull is still there. Moreover, there is a crack in my skull that runs from that hole to the top of my head and from that hole to the bridge of my nose. The deer hunting *arrow had not only made a hole in my head, it made a huge crack.*

So what's to be learned from this experience?

First, consider the risk when you do something like hiding behind a tree in the middle of the yard where most of the arrows come down. I saw this as an opportunity to make more money than the other kids – and I did. But then I ended up in the hospital because of it. I did make $93.00 while in the hospital…. Still, the risk was high and had the arrow struck me one inch lower, in one of my eyes, it would likely have killed me. On top of that, I bet my parents had to pay a lot of money for the hospital bill.

Second, never underestimate the generosity or kindness of your parents' friends – those kind ladies who visited me in the hospital and donated to my cigar box savings. Each was so friendly, generous, and concerned for my health. But equally important, they were also friends of my parents.

Third, don't play stupid games that could cost you your life. Don't pretend to be superman and jump off the second floor of an apartment building thinking you might fly, and don't put yourself in harm's way by catching arrows from a sixteen-year-old boy who should not be shooting them in your direction anyway.

Be thankful for your life and take care of it. And think about the dangers you bring upon yourself. It is not always a life or death situation, often it's a quality of life situation. Try walking on one leg for a day and you will know what it feels like to be in an accident that cost you a leg. Try getting such a hit in your eye that you lose vision and can't see anything from that eye. This actually happened to me and was the result of a chainsaw accident where a large chip of wood hit me in the eye. Three months later, I lost vision in that eye and had to undergo surgery to restore it. Thank goodness for Dr. Brar from the Medical College of Virginia and the McGuire Veterans Hospital in Richmond, Virginia and for the skills he brought to the operating table. If it had not been for such skilled medical care, I would have never regained that vision. And sadly, the whole thing could have been avoided if I had just worn the safety goggles that fogged up and which I hung on a tree limb as I continued to work with the chainsaw.

Failure to use reasonable caution as you go through life can create pain where there doesn't need to be any pain.

Use caution and take care of yourself.

Mischievous Stories

Chapter Two – Electricity

There was money to be made and I needed some of it. Little did I know it would almost cost me my life at age thirteen....

"Have you heard?" asked Billy. "We can gather pinecones and sell them as long as they are green and have not opened. There is a company that is willing to pay us $1.25 per bushel."

"You're kidding," I said. "We live in the state of Georgia and there are thousands of pine trees. Why would anyone want to buy pinecones?" "Besides," I continued, "they are up on the top of the pine trees until they get mature and they open and drop their seeds on the ground."

I recall that when I was in elementary school, every year on Arbor Day each student would be given three one-foot-long pine trees to take home. Arbor Day was the one day per year when everyone was encouraged to plant at least one tree. They were normally wrapped in moist newspaper so they would live a few days and hopefully the children would take them home and plant them with their parents.

"So I guess we would just climb the trees or use ladders to knock down the green pine cones, right?" I suggested to Billy.

"Yup," said Billy. "Then we pick them up and when we get a few bushels we carry them to the place across town where they buy them, and we collect our cash."

Now, a bushel is about two paper grocery bags full to the top with hard, small, green pinecones, many of which were too high in the tree to be knocked down with our broomsticks while we were on the ground. Using a ladder was not too practical because you would have to climb down and reposition the ladder all the time, and even then, you could not get very high on the tree. But sticks were all we had to knock down the cones – oh well.

"My daddy has a boat trailer that has a wooden bed in it and we could use it to haul the pine cones to market," I said.

Our boat trailer doubled as a cargo trailer. It had a box built on the top and you could take the ends of the box out if you were hauling our fifteen-foot-long wooden "john boat." If you put the end slats into the back and front of the wooden box, it became a cargo-hauling trailer for dirt, manure, or – in a perfect world – pinecones.

Our plan was to pick pinecones and, once we filled the trailer with enough of them, we would hook it to the car and carry it to the point of sales on the other side of town and collect our cash in exchange for the pinecones. What a deal!

So, with that discussion and plan of action, Billy and I set out to make our fortune in the pinecone business. It was a short-lived career since nature would eventually open the pinecones and cause the seeds to fall out onto the ground, germinate, and become small pine trees in a matter of months.

The intent of the company that was buying the green pinecones was to get them early and run them through a heater of some kind. The pinecones, when heated correctly, would open and then they would shake the seeds out of the cones and into a container. Then the seeds were carefully planted in rich soil and in a controlled environment like a greenhouse. Soon, new sprouts were finding their way from under the rich moist soil and up toward the sunlight as tiny pine trees.

Giving them to elementary school students was not the only way to distribute them. They also sold them to "tree farmers" who planted the trees and watched them grow for many years until they became large trees that could be harvested. Just look around and see how many wooden telephone poles you see in your neighborhood or city. Most, if not all, are pine trees that have been cut down, the bark removed (and sold to homeowners and landscape companies to be placed in yards across America). Many of the larger, mostly straight trees, become telephone poles.

Tree farmers have fancy machines and they prepare the soil by clearing a big field of all shrubs and small trees and then plowing the ground and making rows. They then put their small trees into the ground and either hope for enough rain to nurture them to life or water them with huge irrigation systems to give them the water they need to grow.

"Let's start today," said Billy. "We can get our feet wet on some trees down on Wilson Avenue and see how much time it takes to collect our first bushel."

"Great idea. I will find a bucket or basket and we can go to work. I guess we will use broomsticks to knock them out of the tree," I commented.

Off we went for our first gathering of pinecones. The work went well but we soon found that our ninth-grade education and ninth grader heights were not enough. We needed to get farther up in the tree to harvest enough pinecones to make it worth the effort. So, a climbing we must go…. Up into the tree we went and soon there were more pinecones on the ground than we could count.

Before we would pick the pinecones, Billy and I had to ask the homeowners if they objected to our climbing the trees and knocking down the pinecones.

"Good morning, sir," I said to the nice man who answered the door, presumably the homeowner.

"Good morning young man," responded the man at the door.

"My friend and I are working to raise money and wondered if we could pick the pinecones from your trees. We will clean up the yard when we are done, and you will have fewer pinecones that open and fall, so you will not have to pick up as many pinecones," I continued.

"Sure," said the kind man. "Just be sure you rake up any mess you might make and be careful not to get hurt."

"Thank you, sir," I said. "We will be careful, and we will clean up before we leave."

And with that, a new enterprise began – pinecone pickers were ready to go to work, almost.

We started with "low-hanging fruit"—the pinecones we could reach and hit with a broomstick or small wooden pole. We probably knocked out about three yards using that method; however, as with all budding enterprises, innovation drove some changes in the technique and there were some *opportunities to improve the process. And improvements meant more effective picking, and more effective picking meant more money.*

The innovation, in this case, was simple. Get a better stick.

Most of the pinecones grew in small clusters of two to four, and these clusters were almost always near the end of the limbs on the pine tree. They were hard as rocks, green in color, and when hit just right fell easily from the tree. There was no need to clip them with pruning shears or anything like that, just a good hit from a stick was enough to knock them off the tree limb and onto the ground below.

Billy's father was a kind man, and I was always welcome at their home. He was also an important man in the industry of our small town in South Georgia. Important because he was the president, chief executive officer, or chief operating officer of the aluminum manufacturer in Tifton. It was a pretty large plant and employed a lot of people, and they could make all kinds of things from aluminum.

"Look what my Dad got for us!" exclaimed Billy after showing me a ten-foot-long aluminum pole. It was lightweight, longer than the broomstick handles we had been using, and we could reach out to the end of the tree limbs and hit those clusters of cones faster and with more effectiveness than when we had

to climb out onto the limb. The provision of these poles also helped us work safer as we could stay near the trunk of the tree and have less chance of a tree limb breaking and us falling out of the tree. It was a perfect solution.

Next to silver, copper, and gold, aluminum is a metal that is best at conducting electricity. Silver is the very best, then copper, then pure gold, and then aluminum. Aluminum is also very light, and when extruded into a pipe that is hollow in the middle, it does not rust or bend easily. The aluminum poles provided by Billy's dad made a great replacement for a wooden broomstick or cane fishing pole we were using.

These ten-foot poles turned out to be an effective, efficient, and free solution to our short pole problem, and we were glad to have them.

"Let's go down on Park Avenue today," said Billy. And off we went with poles in hand.

We were enterprising high-school freshmen who found the ninth grade more than exciting in 1968. But like all high-school kids, we needed money, and our parents taught us that you had to work to make money, and so work we did.

"Let's tackle that tree," I said. It was a large, tall pine next to a paved road near the intersection of 22nd Street and Park Avenue in Tifton, Georgia. My

cousin, Jack, came along that day to hang out with us and helped us on the ground, gathering the cones we were able to knock down out of the tree.

The aluminum poles were outstanding. They helped us knock down the cones at the end of the limbs, and our production went up because we could knock down many more cones than when we just had the wooden poles or when we shook the tree limb to get the cones to fall.

In a T-shirt, shorts, and with no shoes, I climbed the tree. Billy was similarly dressed, and up he went too. The cones fell like huge raindrops, often bouncing from one tree limb to the other as they plummeted to the ground. Each one that hit the ground was worth about a penny, and we filled bushel baskets with ease. A penny per cone does not sound like much, but you must put it in perspective: fifteen cents would buy a bottle of Coke in those days or a candy bar. Just a few years before it was ten cents, and a few before that, it was six cents for a Coke. Gas was about 33 cents per gallon. Today, the prices are much higher.

Our parents did not charge us to haul a load of cones to the marketplace, and we reused the baskets in which we collected the cones. The poles were provided by Billy's dad at no charge. So profit was 100% because costs were zero – except, of course, for the time we spent knocking down the cones and collecting them off the ground. Those labor costs were split, and the money made was divided evenly between me and Billy.

"Check it out," I said, "we have already knocked down about two bushels of cones and we have only been working for a few minutes."

"Yup," said Billy, "this is a good tree," as he climbed about fifteen feet higher than me.

I settled into a spot about the height of the top wire on the telephone and power lines that ran down the side of Park Avenue.

As pine trees grow, they shed their lower limbs. In 1968, when we climbed the pine tree, the lowest limbs were only five or six feet from the ground and there were many limbs between the ground and the top of the tree.   Most of these limbs had pinecones on them. Some of those limbs, however, grew into the power lines, and the power company or the city workers had to come by and trim them back. But in Tifton, Georgia, in 1968, there were a lot of pine trees and not nearly enough city workers to keep all the limbs trimmed away from the power lines.

It was true then, and may still be true today, that the very top power line on a telephone pole is normally not insulated. Most of the wires you see today in the home are covered with rubber and therefore safer to touch. This rubber coating is called *insulation. But uninsulated power lines carry the highest voltage of electricity. It's part of something called "the grid" that carries electricity from our power production plants across America and into our homes, factories, and businesses.*

I told Billy, "I'm going to stop right here," as he continued further up the tree.

Almost immediately, we were being productive. The aluminum poles were doing the trick. Lightweight, easy to handle, and strong. But then there was that thing about being a great conductor of electricity. And there was that thing about the power line at the top of the telephone poles that ran from one pole to the next with absolutely no rubber to insulate. And there were those tree limbs that had grown over the years into the power lines and all this was complicated by the fact that the city and power company did not have enough workers to trim all those limbs back. It was a formula for disaster.

This mixture of circumstances created an opportunity for danger that was not apparent at first glance.

I grasped the aluminum pole like a person grips a golf club. My right hand held the pole at the end closest to me and my left hand was wrapped around the end of the right hand. Much like playing miniature golf. The pole extended out about ten feet.

I leaned my right shoulder against the trunk of the tree and sat gently on a limb to stabilize myself. My right bare foot connected with a tree limb as I pushed the pole into a cluster of pinecones. One foot was in the air, and one on a tree limb. Direct hit. Down they fell. Then another cluster of cones, and they fell. Then another and another. But my aim was not always perfect. Sometimes I would miss the cluster and the pole would drop down a few feet, only to be pulled back and a second attempt made to knock down that cluster of cones.

As I lunged with my pole at a cluster of cones, I missed the cones and the pole fell a bit, bouncing off the power line. The power line made a twinging noise like hitting a single key on the piano keyboard. I have since heard electrical workers talk about the power lines "singing" to them. I know this noise. But, no harm, no foul, just try it again.

The next time when I lunged for that cluster of cones, I missed again. But this time, the highly conductive aluminum pole landed on the power line and sat there….

A jolt of electricity immediately hit me! I felt my hands and body shaking. But they were not really shaking, just the nerves in my body were rattling like a spoon in a glass that is vibrating aggressively. Or like when you are really cold and shivering and your teeth shake so bad that they click together. That's what it felt like.

Electricity is strange, and when you get really high voltages of electricity it paralyzes the body. The nerves that normally help our brain make our muscles move were going crazy. I knew I had to let go of the pole, but I could not. My brain was sending the signals to the muscles through the nervous system, but the muscles would not respond correctly. They would not obey! I was in trouble. I was paralyzed!

Although I was paralyzed, I focused my thoughts on letting go of the aluminum pole in my hand. "How hard could this be?" I thought to myself. "Just let it go". But my hands would not respond. Nothing I could do, and no amount of concentration, would allow me to let go of that efficient conductor of high-voltage electricity. But the problem was worse than that: I could not breathe.

Life is short when you can't breathe. Our body needs the oxygen that our lungs provide. When we don't get oxygen, we panic and do everything we can to get some air into our lungs, so the lungs can provide oxygen to our body. Just try holding your breath. You can do it for a little while, but not for very long.

But to breathe, our nervous system must work with our brain and our muscles so that our chest expands, and the air is drawn into our lungs. When high-voltage electricity paralyzes your body, and the nerves and muscles do not work together, you are in serious trouble.

It took only a few moments for me to realize that I was going to die because I could not breathe.

Billy was above me in the tree, I could not call for help since I was paralyzed by the huge amount of electrical voltage that came from the power line, through my aluminum pole, into my body and then through the tree and into the ground. I could not make noise of any significant level, although I seemed to be able to groan just a bit but with very little volume. I was going to die!

I grew up attending the First United Methodist Church in my hometown. I knew about God, and as I realized that my death was imminent, I prayed that God would comfort my family and friends and forgive me of my sins, like throwing tomatoes at the neighbors' door or ringing the doorbell and running away….

When I finished my prayer, a great peace came over me and I knew everything would be OK. I remember thinking about my death and being sad that my mother would miss me, but I knew that everyone else would be fine. I knew that I was safe and that I would be fine too.

Smoke began to rise from below in front of my face. It came from over my shoulder too and the modest wind pushed it into my peripheral vision. That's the vision you can see out of the corner of your eyes. It's like watching home plate from the pitcher's mound and you can still see a bit of movement on third or first base.

I decided that the tree was on fire. I didn't really think much about it because as the smoke rose the oxygen in my body was about gone. It had been only a minute or two, but I was not able to breathe.

As the oxygen provided by my lungs was not being replenished, my body must have begun to shut down. Almost like turning off a computer. There is an orderly process for the shutdown of a computer and a somewhat orderly process for the shutdown of a human body. The last thing I remember was seeing Billy's pole fly by between me and the power line. He had apparently discovered that I was in trouble and decided to throw his pole at my pole in an attempt to break the connection between me and the power line.

He missed.

My next memory was of Billy as he sat or stood on a limb behind me. I am not sure how much time transpired between the time the pole came flying by and the time I heard Billy talking to me. However, during that time, Billy had climbed down from his higher location in the tree and, knowing that if he touched my pole he would likely be electrocuted, he made a wiser choice. Billy reached out for a limb that he could pull back and then position the limb in a spot where, when released, it would swing forward and push the pole off the power line or out of my hands. It worked! The pole fell to the ground and my connection to the electrical voltage from that high-voltage power line was broken. Immediately, I could breathe again.

"You have a really big hole in your back," said Billy. Oh no, I now began to realize that the smoke I had seen was not the tree burning—it was me!

"It's good to be alive again," I replied.

Not much was said as we climbed down the pine tree to the ground. My cousin, Jack, was helping us that day. He saw me and ran next door, where my mother was visiting her friend. We were only a couple of blocks away from my home. I noticed that my right foot was black with charred skin. I didn't really realize it, much less understand why, but my right shoulder had been burned too. There was a hole about a quarter of an inch deep and about as big around as a baseball and both the shoulder and the foot looked like burned pieces of chicken on the BBQ grill. Gross!

But the good news was, there was no pain. Nothing hurt. So, I walked next door and my mother came running out the front door to see about me. She called my doctor and he agreed to meet us at the hospital. In the 1958 Ford we jumped, and off to the hospital we drove. What happened at the hospital is still a mystery to me. I seem to remember the doctors cleaning up my wounds, but I think they had given me some pain medication because I don't remember much about the first few hours at the hospital.

The next thing I knew, I was lying in a hospital bed in a light blue gown. My dad came into the room and my mother was there too. I was still in no pain, but I had bandages on my right shoulder and on my right foot and everyone was very concerned about me. There were no burns on my hands as the newspaper reported.

I lay in that hospital bed for five days. Billy came to visit me, but my parents informed me that I was out of the pinecone picking business. Still, the picture we took that day ended up in The Tifton Gazette newspaper and Billy and I remained friends for years. Truly, Billy had saved my life. If not for him, I would have burned to death in the top of that pine tree.

Each day I was in the hospital, my bandages were changed. I seem to remember that the doctors were not quite certain how to proceed with my treatment. As it turns out the reason there was no pain had to do with the nerves in my foot and back being dead. Apparently, electricity can kill the nerves in your body. It did so to mine. In the beginning, I don't think the doctor knew if he would have to cut off part of my foot or not. Turns out, I got to keep my foot and all my toes.

Soon I was allowed to leave the hospital and finish my recovery at home. My Aunt Helen, Jack's mother, was a registered nurse, and each day she came to our house and checked my wounds, changed the bandages, and made sure that I was healing well

This occurred daily for many weeks as my wounds got better. Her care and concern for me was genuine and her nursing skills saved the day. I had to go to school on wooden crutches for several weeks, but I healed well and soon found myself running again and playing as if nothing had happened.

I was very fortunate that Billy was in the tree with me and that we were working as a team. If it had not been for Billy's smart and quick thinking, I would have died on that day and in that tree. Teamwork is important in many aspects of life. Each person on the team bring capabilities that might not be as strong in another person, but those capabilities make the team much stronger. Picking the right team member or buddy is often a personal choice and a very important choice. In this case, it was by chance and by choice. If you hang out with the wrong friends, the results could be bad. If, however, you surround yourself with good people and good friends who work hard and contribute to the team in a meaningful way, it might just save your life.

Newspaper Article Courtesy of the Newnan Times-Herald, (October 10, 1968)

Former Newnan Youth Saves Life of Friend

Quick action by 12-year-old Billy Koran, of Tifton, formerly of Newnan, saved the life of a friend who was almost electrocuted last week in Tifton.

David Merritt, 13, is recovering in Tift General Hospital from burns. He might have been dead if it had not been for Billy Koran.

Young Merritt was using a long aluminum pole last Thursday to knock pine cones from trees when the pole touched a high voltage utility line. He was unable to relax his grip on the pole.

Koran, reacting quickly, grabbed a big stick and knocked the pole out of Merritt's hands. The boy had severe burns on his hands, but apparently suffered no other injuries. Doctors said he was lucky to be alive.

Billy Koran is the son of Mr. and Mrs. Frank Koran, formerly of Newnan.

As you go through life, you will decide who your friends are. This is a choice over which you normally have complete control. I am fortunate Billy Koran was my friend. Others may have let me burn to death in that tree, but not Billy.

Pick good friends!

Mischievous Stories

41

Chapter Three – Snake Pond

I've said it before and I'll say it again, growing up in "Small Town USA" has advantages and disadvantages. One of the disadvantages is that most small towns don't have a lot of kid-friendly activities to do. There are not multiple instances of bowling alleys, skating rinks, go-cart tracks, golf courses, or in my days, video arcades. In fact, when I was growing up, video games did not exist. No fancy handheld devices, no cell phones, no laptop or desktop computers, and no Wi-Fi networks. Our TV was black and white and only had three channels. So when you wanted to have fun, it was almost always outside and almost always created by the boys and girls who lived in the neighborhood in which you grew up.

In my hometown of Tifton, Georgia, there was a bowling alley and a roller-skating rink. However, I don't think my parents ever took us bowling. Tifton had a swimming pool, and my parents made sure we knew how to swim as soon as we were old enough to take swimming lessons. It cost 25 cents to go to the pool, but it was not always open when we wanted to go swimming, although we used it a lot when it was open and the weather was good for outdoor swimming. But when that was not the case, there was always Tift Pond, Fulwood Pond, and then we "created" Snake Pond.

Farming was one of the main ways of making money in the South. The climate and waterfall each year were pretty good and enabled a long growing season during which farmers would plant their crops, water and fertilize them, and then harvest their crops. While the rain was normally sufficient for the crops, there was often a need to water the crops during the summer when it was really hot and there just was not enough rain. For that reason, farmers dug holes in the ground and God filled them with water when it rained. They were normally not very deep, perhaps six to eight feet or so. Toward the edge of the pond, it got shallower.

When I first visited this pond with my friends Terry, Tommy, Everette, and my brother Fred, we were focused on exploring. We looked around the woods surrounding the pond and just checked out the area with no real purpose in mind. Later, we decided to go skinny dipping. Skinny dipping is swimming in a pond or pool in only your birthday suit. Another way to describe this is to say that we swam butt naked. We would put our clothes on the ground and run into the pond naked for a swim. It was just four or five boys, eight to twelve years old, and we didn't think anything about it. We had a wonderful time playing in the water, splashing around as you would in a swimming pool if you had 25 cents and the pool was open. But when we didn't have the money or when we just happened to be down by the pond and the urge to swim hit us, we just threw our shorts, shirts, shoes – if we had them on – to the ground at the end of the pond and in we went into the water. We thought nothing of it, but the farmer did!

Soon, over the hill came a pickup truck with a dust trail behind it and it was moving fast. It was a person I referred to as "Farmer Jones." His name was not Mr. Jones, but that's the name I gave him. We didn't know his real name. And when he came barreling across the field toward the pond, we knew it was not going to be a friendly visit. The first time, he just told us to get out of the pond and go home and that it was dangerous for us to swim in that pond. We did what he said; however, that did not mean we never intended to swim there again. After all, this was fun. The water was cool, and we had a wonderful time swimming. We did not see the danger. In fact, the danger was slithering all around us, by the hundreds…. Snakes!

What Farmer Jones said was so true. We didn't have floats to play on, so the next best thing was a log. One day, in the sizzling summer sun, I decided to drag a log into the pond. As I walked across the dam on the modest road that was on top of it, I turned left at the end and entered an area that had tall grass and lots of bushes. Along the edge of the pond were some logs from fallen dead trees. I picked one and began the process of moving it into the water. As I turned it over, I was shocked to see two cottonmouth water moccasins. I jumped back away from the log, yelled "snake!" and started looking for a stick the size of a small baseball bat and about as big around with which I could kill the two snakes.

Cottonmouth water moccasins are called "cottonmouth" because the inside of their mouth is white. They are pit vipers. That means they have heat-sensing pits in their face between their eyes and nose. These pits help the snake sense temperatures. So if you stick your hand out or walk by a moccasin, its senses the heat from your hand or foot and strikes out to bite what it thinks might harm them or what it might think it can eat.

The poor mouse that passes in front of a pit viper is likely to become dinner. Ouch.

The other reason that a snake will strike is from fear. When backed down, they wrap their body into a coil and then, when they decide to do so, they push out toward the object they intend to bite as they open their mouth. Two huge fangs come out, and when they clamp their fangs into a hand, ankle, mouse, or another animal, the fangs inject venom into the object they bite. This venom kills their prey or the poor swimmer that caused them fear and causes them to strike.

Farmer Jones was right; this place was dangerous.

With club in hand, I killed the two snakes under the log. They were only about a foot long and kind of small. But where there are children, mama is not far behind. Such is the case with people—and with snakes.

Soon we were turning over all the logs around the pond and killing all the snakes we could. Killing them made our swimming safer, and while we still had an inherent fear of snakes, we somehow felt enabled to eradicate as many snakes as we could. During the two or three years we swam in snake pond, we must have killed well over a hundred snakes. It became an easy task, but a very dangerous one. A mean snake would do what's necessary to protect its domain. But the good news is that they didn't look for a fight. If you wanted to fight with a snake, you had to go after them or come so close to them that they felt threatened and would strike out with large fangs full of and ready to push venom from their body into yours.

One afternoon, Terry and Fred led us around the back side of the pond, far from the dam, and we left dry land, walking along the top of a fallen tree that rested about half in the water and half out of the water. It was flat and level; the limbs had long ago died or broken off. For us, it worked well as a bridge. The total length was only about ten feet.

Fred and Terry were already across the eight-inch-wide bridge, with Everette following. I was behind Everette. When I got within a foot or two of dry land on the distant side of this makeshift bridge, I saw something in the water. Now, the water was only six to eight inches deep, and it was relatively clear. You could see a sandy kinda bottom of the pond with some green vegetation growing in the sunlit water. You could also see an object that looked like it didn't belong.

When I spotted that object, Everette had already stepped off the log and onto dry land.

"Everette, come back here and look at this," I said.

"What is it?" Everette responded as he came back to the log.

"I'm not sure, but I think it's a snake, see what you think," I told him as both of us bent over to get a closer look at the snake. He was about two feet long, and about as big around as a magic marker. Jake, as I later learned to call him (a quick reference to "Jake the Snake"), was coiled and ready to strike. His head was about two inches below the surface of the water.

I bent down as low as I could and got within about a foot of the water. The more I looked at the object coiled below and well blended into the sandy soil below the water's surface, the more I was convinced it was a snake.

After studying the object for about fifteen seconds, I decided it must be a snake. I stood up and darn near jumped off the log and onto the land near where Everette was standing. I was scared. I also knew I had stuck my face within striking distance of Jake the Snake, and he could have struck at any moment.

I grabbed a nearby stick that was about four feet long and stuck it in the water near Jake. Sure enough, like a toy with a new battery, Jake came alive. He was probably as scared as I was, but at this point, I had the upper hand, and in my hand was a stick with which I could have killed him.

But rather than swim toward me, Jake started out in the other direction and headed away from Everette and me. He swam fast, and his motions were like a very prolific "S" as he propelled himself along the top of the water and away from the four of us. Jake was fortunate and so were we! He lived to swim another day, and we went on our way down the farm road, past the farmer's house and towards our home on Murray Avenue.

I too was fortunate. I had engaged in some pretty foolish behavior that could have easily gotten me killed or injured. Willful disobedience to the farmer's wishes by swimming in that dangerous place with all those snakes was foolish. We gave no thought to it, but it is a wonder that we did not get bitten by one of the snakes. And in this last interaction with the snake under the water, my face was inches from a coiled cottonmouth water moccasin that could have easily bitten me in the face.

As I walked away, I realized how lucky I was and how close I was to death or serious injury. Later in life, I realized that I took a risk that I should not have taken. Avoiding risks helps ensure success.

And as you learn to make decisions, be certain that you look at each situation you are in and decide if the risk of something bad happening to you is worth enjoyment you get from that activity.

Sometimes it is not, and you should find something else to do.

Mischievous Stories

Chapter Four – Prowling

We were about twelve years old and camping out in the backyard was kind of an exciting thing to do from spring through the fall of that year in South Georgia. We enjoyed the opportunity for friends to come over and frequently would camp in our backyard or across the alley in the backyard adjacent to ours and owned by Terry Payne's parents. Oftentimes we would build a fire out of wood we gathered from around the neighborhood. We would sit around the campfire and enjoy the freedoms that we were experiencing as young boys hanging out in the neighborhood. We often lay on a farm trailer in Tommy's backyard and looked up at the sky for shooting stars. It was really a pretty great life.

On most nights, we would roam the streets a little bit and we would almost always go to the Royal Castle Restaurant about two miles from our house and have a hamburger and a Royal Cola and then come back. At the Royal Castle you could buy twelve silver-dollar-size hamburgers for a buck. We never really did any damage or harm to anyone or anything, but we did stay out on the streets after curfew. In our small town, that was at 11 o'clock for boys and girls under sixteen years old.

Mischievous Stories

The sound of the whistle could be heard for miles and miles as one of the many freight trains passed through our town each night. Often, we would lay a penny or nickel on the train track and the train wheels would smash the coin flat. Mr. Lincoln's head would be flat, and his hair would be a bit messed up after thousands and thousands of pounds rolled over the coin and the pressure of the train would spit the coin out into the middle of the train tracks amongst the wooden cross members that held the rails of the track in place.

Back in those days, there was a lot of mischief for country boys to get into. Putting cherry bombs in Farmer Jones' chicken coop drew his anger and on one occasion drew his shotgun. As Terry dove over the fence, Farmer Jones fired and Terry's butt was pelted with several pieces of salt. This was not the first time he had awoken to the sound of angry chickens who were victims of mischief. Farmer Jones knew we would be back. He removed the buckshot out of a shotgun shell and filled it with rock salt. It would hurt like heck, but at least it was not steel pellets getting shot into your body. Terry's mother had to lay him face-down on the coffee table at home and pull out the salt pellets from his butt with her tweezers.

I am told that some of the kids blew up mailboxes. I never did, but some did. That was a federal crime and not one I wanted to be involved in.

Of course, you could ring someone's doorbell at 1:00 a.m. and run just far enough to see them come to the door and be furious that they had been awaken at such an early hour. And then there were the parkers. Parkers were teenagers with cars that would come down to our neck of the woods near the end of town where roads were being cut and neighborhoods were being built and park. They would normally park on the dark dirt roads, cut through what once was a cow pasture, and kiss their girls while watching the stars. We would sneak up to the back of the car and jump on the bumper and then run into the pecan orchard next to the road. It was all in fun.

Lastly, there were eggs, which had been left on this earth by chickens and delivered to our refrigerators by parents. None of us came out on Friday or Saturday nights without a couple of eggs to use down on 20th Street. You see, there was a drop-off, like the edge of a cliff, from the yards next to 20th Street and between Murray and Wilson Avenues. From three feet above the road, one could rear back and make the pitch of your life with an egg that would hit the side of a car and smash. Now, the real fun in this was not harming someone or messing up their car, it was when you hit some teenager's truly hot Ford Mustang – a Mustang that had been washed and polished for a weekend date with his girl. For those cars, the drivers would often slam on the brakes, throw the transmission in reverse, burn rubber backing up, and turn into the alley in an effort to catch the boys throwing the eggs. But they never did.

Now, boys in South Georgia often roamed around during warm days in shorts, T-shirts, and often without shoes. That was the case with me. But the challenge of no shoes often presented itself in the form of injuries. Nails in the foot, stickers, or a bruise from a rock as you played tag or baseball or some other outdoor sport. Most often, the rule of the day was to get outside and play and be home before the streetlights come on.

So, camping out was an opportunity for great fun, some mischievous excitement, some camaraderie around a fire, and some chats in the small pup tents our parents had given us. Mostly it was innocent fun mixed with an occasional swim in the local college swimming pool or a climb up the college water tower to paint your initials or even your name.

Little did we know that night that we would have so much excitement. But for some reason, I had a wound of some sort on my foot and I couldn't go prowling that evening. Roaming the streets and visiting the Royal Castle was not fun when your foot hurt. However, my friend Everett and my brother Fred went prowling while I stayed in the tent and sacked out a little earlier than I normally would have. Our tent was in the corner of our backyard, between a fig tree and a pear tree. Both produced good fruit and provided nourishment for the bees.

It was a little after midnight, as the police drove down Highway 41 toward 20th Street, they saw Fred in a phone booth. "Police!" Fred and Everette yelled almost simultaneously to each other, and they both started to run. Everett took refuge in the water in the creek almost directly under the phone booth. Fred ran past the convenient store and down a steep hill. At the bottom of that hill was the same creek Everette was hiding in. If you knew exactly when to jump – and we had been down that hill a million times and knew exactly where to place our foot and exactly when to jump – you could clear the creek and stay dry, landing on the grass behind what was then a putt-putt golf course and later a bank drive-through ATM.

Yes indeed, you could jump right over that creek and keep on going past the putt-putt and into the woods. Once inside those woods, we had in-depth knowledge of the trails that led through those woods, and nobody could have found Fred or Everette. In that area, if the police were chasing you or some other boys were chasing you, they would never find you because we knew exactly where we were going, and they wouldn't. Once in the woods, you could lay low and just wait for the police to go away.

Fred tells a story that he jumped the ditch and had run about halfway through the lot containing the putt-putt only to think to himself, "Why am I running? I didn't do anything wrong." He stopped dead in his tracks and waited for the policeman to catch up. The policeman, however, wasn't so fortunate. He didn't know exactly where to place his foot, he probably didn't even know there was a small creek at the bottom of that hill, and he certainly didn't know where to jump so that he didn't end up in the creek. So, the creek is exactly where he ended up.

His uniform was soaked from the knees down, and he had some mud on his uniform. His shoes filled quickly with water. His pistol had gotten wet, as did the ammunition, his flashlight, handcuffs, and other equipment on his belt. The ditch was only probably four feet wide and about a foot or two feet deep, depending on how much rain there had been. It was a small creek, but if you didn't jump it, you were going to get wet, and he did get wet. So the officer was angry when he caught up with Fred.

"Why did you run?" asked the officer of my brother.

"I don't know," said Fred, "I was just scared."

The officers put my brother in the police car and brought him home, and Everett ran the four blocks, after he came up out of the water, to our house. Everett had submerged himself in that creek and hidden from the police in a culvert that crossed under the road and through which the creek ran. When he got to my tent in our backyard, he was soaked, tired, and out of breath.

"Wake up, wake up, the police have picked up Fred!" said Everette. I couldn't imagine what he would have done wrong to have been picked up by the police except that just being out at that time of night was a crime punishable by bringing you home and waking your parents up. You see, in those days the police didn't carry young boys to the police station and put them in jail. Instead, they would simply carry you home to your parents. As most of us in the South

know, that can be far worse than going to the police station.

Anyway, I poked my head out of the tent just in time to hear my mother say, "Now Fred, I would have expected something like this out of David, but I'm surprised at you." My brother was not so innocent, but I had a bit of a reputation for being a little more outgoing and perhaps a little wilder than he was. I was the smallest kid in the neighborhood and sometimes that meant I got bullied, so I had to have a tougher shell than the other boys! And perhaps I was a bit more mischievous. Fine. Whatever.

When the police left, my brother and I had to go inside and to bed – in the house. The next morning, we had a discussion with our parents. We talked about what was perceived to be my behavior and Fred's behavior the previous night. But, in reality, it was Everett's behavior and my brother Fred's behavior that night. I was not prowling with my brother; Everett was.

The punishment for those high crimes and misdemeanors was no camping out anymore, period. Forever and ever, amen. It didn't matter that I didn't do anything, and even though I said it wasn't me, they didn't believe me, and they didn't ask who it was. I didn't want to rat out Everett, so I took that punishment just as if I had committed the crime. Everett continued to enjoy camping out for the balance of the spring, summer, and fall. Unfortunately, Fred and I did not get to join him. No more camping in the backyard or in the neighbor's yard behind the alley across the street. No more campfires. It was not fair to me. Fred deserved it, but I did not!

I spent about a year resenting this punishment and angry about the idea that I couldn't camp out and that I was being punished for something that I didn't do. It is true that, had my foot not been hurting that night, I would have been right there with them. But the fact is, I wasn't.

As the story is told to me, Fred was in a phone booth when the police started coming down the street. You see, we would always check the phone booth to see if there was a dime in the pay phone, left by some adult in too big a rush to wait for the phone to remit a dime for an incomplete call. Back then, you could buy a Coca-Cola, Orange Crush, root beer, or grape soda for a dime in the machine at the convenience store not too far down the street. It would also buy five pieces of gum.

Fred and I suffered through that next year of no camping, but one spring day the next year, I really wanted to camp out. I decided in a moment of anger and tears that I was being punished for something I shouldn't be punished for.

I went to my father and I said, "I want to camp out. I was not out prowling with Fred when the police picked him up. It was Everett who was with him. I was in the tent the whole time." I appealed to my father's sense of fairness to be allowed to camp out again, and he granted that permission to both of us, and we both got to camp out again.

I learned a lesson or two out of that event. The first lesson was, "Don't take the blame for something you didn't do." There's plenty of blame to go around for all the things that people do, but there's no sense in taking the blame for something you didn't do. That is what I had done that year. I regretted it, but it seemed like the right thing at the time. However, at the end of the day, I was very unhappy with the results of my accepted punishment that I didn't deserve. The second lesson was, "Be cautious what you do in life that might get you into trouble and follow you for a good bit of your adult life." What if one of those thrown eggs had hit a driver in the head as he or she drove down 20th Street with a window down? Someone could have been killed or badly hurt over a stupid joke. What if I had thrown an egg at a police car by mistake and he was patrolling with his window down. If the egg had hit the officer, it might have been felony assault on a police officer. What if I got caught painting my name on the Abraham Baldwin Agricultural College water tower and had to pay for it to be painted from top to bottom? Both were powerful lessons.

In the army we used to say, "The commander is responsible for everything his unit does or fails to do." Well, that's the truth, and unfortunately, sometimes your people will do things that surprise you and disappoint you, and in certain leadership positions, you're simply responsible for that too – as unfair as it may be.

As unfair as not getting to camp out was for me, it was my punishment for not speaking up, for not defending myself, and for taking the blame for something I didn't do.

But this story isn't over just yet.

Little did Fred know when he was returned home by the police that night that he would grow up and join the United States Army. But he did. He joined the army, completed training as a military policeman, and was transferred to Germany, where he served for several years. When he came back to America, he was stationed in New York City. Later, he decided to leave the army. He left with great skills. He knew the law, he knew how to treat people, and he knew how to make really important decisions that could have an impact on someone's life for years and years.

Fred moved back to the City of Tifton, Georgia, where he became a deputy sheriff. As is normally the case, a veteran officer was assigned to train him in his duties as a deputy and to ride with him for some period of time until he learned his duties on the civilian side of law enforcement.

Well, as luck might have it, it was the same deputy who chased him down that steep hill next to the convenience store near the corner of Highway 41 and 20th Street. Yup, the same person who fifteen years earlier had chased him down the hill and had run into the creek at the bottom of the hill. Isn't it interesting how things happen in life?

Fred served the citizens of Tifton, Georgia, with the sheriff's department for several years, and then moved to North Georgia, where he became a policeman on a college campus that was part of the University of Georgia. Fortunately, he never had to chase a person into a creek at the bottom of a hill.

Once I had a friend who decided to go down a wrong path. His path was criminal. He initially set his alarm to get up at 2:00 a.m. so that he could sneak out of his house. Soon, he had conditioned his body to awake at that early hour. Then he began to do really bad things. He would intentionally damage property or go into our high school and rummage around. Soon, his intentions got even worse until one night, he used spray paint to paint all the halls inside our high school. He destroyed televisions, trophy cases, and other items in the school. His behavior was illegal, inappropriate, and unnecessary.

I looked up to a particular policeman in our community. He had a part-time job at a convenience store near our home. Two days after the incident, Officer Jim asked me if I knew anything about the damage that had been done at the school over the weekend. I did. And I told on him that day.

You see, what that boy did harmed everyone. Someone had to pay for all those repairs. Someone had to paint the walls in the school and buy new trophy cases. Sure, we prowled around when we camped out, but we did not destroy things that belonged to others. And when my brother ran from the police that night, he had not done any damage to anything. So, he stopped, thought about what he was doing, and admitted to the police officer that he had made a mistake in running.

There was punishment for that error in judgment but the behavior that caused so much pain was never repeated.

As you go through life, think about the things that you do. I generally don't take the blame for things I didn't do unless the people who did it are working for me and I'm responsible as a manager or a leader, and then I'm to blame. Short of that, people are responsible for their own actions, and hopefully, those actions are not terrible and don't cause great problems to many people.

<u>*You are responsible for what you do*</u> *and, in some cases, for what you fail to do.*

Fred was lucky that the police brought him home instead of taking him to the police stations and booking him for his misconduct.

Remember to follow the rules, obey your parents, question friends who want you to do something that you know you should not.

In the long run, you will be glad you did.

Mischievous Stories

Chapter Five – Alligators in South Georgia

    The house at the end of Murray Avenue in Tifton, Georgia, was a modest home. When we moved in, the road in front and on the side of the house was dirt. It was the last house on our street, and 22nd Street ran alongside our home and intersected with Murray Avenue. I can remember my mother telling her friends who would come to visit that we were the last house on the right on Murray Avenue. Soon after we moved there, that would change, as a very nice subdivision would be built on what was then a cow pasture and pecan orchard. We played baseball in the front yard, had great neighbors that were about our age, and it was a wonderful place to live. There were cows across the street in the huge pecan orchard, but we were not allowed to cross the fence and go into the orchard. No matter which way you went on 22nd street, within three or four blocks, you would find a creek and a place for boys to play in the water.

    Our home had a total of four bedrooms. Two on the right side of the house as you face it, one in the center of the house at the back, and one on the left side of the house. The one on the left side had its own bathroom, bathtub, toilet, and sink, and so it was always reserved for the oldest boy in the family that was living at home. And when an overnight guest came to visit, that room served as our guest room. The oldest boy would have his own room, and the other boys slept together in the middle bedroom on the back side of the house. I was the youngest of the three boys who lived in that house. My brother Marcus was the oldest and Fred was in between.

So, our parents had four boys, Bob, Marcus, Fred, and yours truly. Three of us still lived at home. The oldest boy was my brother Bob. He had finished high school and had joined the United States Navy. He was away at sea. I really do not have any memory of Bob until he came home from the navy in a sharp-looking sailor's uniform. I was impressed. But even though I don't remember him before that, he claims he changed a million of my diapers when I was an infant, and I have seen photos of him driving me around the yard while I sat in the big basket on the front of his bicycle. Lucky for me that there were not four boys around when I was growing up or I would have never had a chance to move into the big bedroom at the end of the house.

In my younger years from age four through ten or so, my brother Fred and I slept in the double bed in the middle bedroom, and my brother Marcus had the room at the end of the house. We had a black and white television with three remote controls. They had names, Marcus, Fred, and David. We had wooden floors and no air conditioning. The summers in South

Georgia were incredibly hot. Marcus was eight years older than me and soon would go off to college. He was lucky. Both Fred and I hoped to get that room when Marcus finished his studies at Abraham Baldwin Agricultural College, commonly known as ABAC, when he left for his last two years of college at the University of Georgia. Fred was only a year older than me, so I thought I might argue that age was not the only consideration when deciding who got the room with the bathroom next to it when Marcus departed. Only time would tell.

One evening I came home from cutting yards – that's how we boys made our spending money until we were old enough to get a real job. I immediately went down to Marcus' room to get a shower. When I pulled the shower curtain back, I was shocked to see a small alligator swimming around in about two inches of water. That alligator scared me a little bit, but I had seen alligators before when we visited the Okefenokee National Wildlife Refuge, a 402,000-acre park in South Georgia.

There were thousands of alligators in the Okefenokee. Sometimes they would swim up right to the edge of your boat. Once, my parents, my brother and I were in a treehouse, built by the national park service, next to one of the creeks, and an alligator swam up next to the boat and would not let us get in our boat. Finally, the big gator swam away. We got in the boat and headed out of there. On another visit, mostly a fishing trip, we had about twenty fish on a stringer in the water when suddenly the water swirled, and all our fish were gone! A gator had eaten every fish we had caught in one huge bite. So disappointing.

The good news was, this alligator in the bathtub was a very small one, and his bite was not even bad, as I later found out. It turns out that someone had brought that gator by the house for my brother Marcus and left it there. My parents elected to put it in the bathtub for safe keeping. Boy was I surprised when I threw back the shower curtain and I was greeted by Mister Gator. They had originally put the alligator in a tub, but not a bathtub. It was a galvanized bucket – a metal bucket that would not rust – in the backyard. Then they decided that for the time being, they would simply put it in the bathtub in the bedroom at the end of the house.

Well, that alligator soon became the family pet for my brother Fred and me, and we enjoyed taking the gator out and playing with him in the front yard. My mother gave us strips of chicken for the gator to eat. Mister Gator played in the front yard, and we would wet him down with the water hose and have a good time with him. He grew quickly. Over the course of two or three weeks, that alligator grew to be about two and a half feet long. He got bigger around, and at first, when he would bite your finger, it didn't hurt.

But as the gator got older and bigger, pretty soon biting down on your finger actually hurt, and his teeth would pierce the skin. So, we were a lot more cautious with him. He had sharp claws on his feet. Gators use them for digging and for traction while they're up on the banks of the rivers, or wherever they might be.

That gator became a pretty good little pet, and all the neighbors came over and were excited to be able to play with a real live alligator. Often, we would carry him down 22nd Street toward the bottom of the hill near Hall Avenue. There was a nice little creek along the way. That creek had an area of about the size of two small cars next to each other. It was between six and twelve inches deep, and it held very clear water. Along the bottom of the creek were rocks, sand, and dirt. You could play in that creek, and it wouldn't get all muddy, so you could almost always see the bottom, and the water would flow through it if it rained. Sometimes if it really rained a lot that creek would get a couple of feet deep, as the rain came through and it went into a culvert, and then down underground.

Well, this particular gator loved to play in that water, and we loved to take him down there. There were crawfish in the water, and there were some *minnows that you would see from time to time, and a few frogs too. The gator never did try and eat the crawfish, frogs, or minnows. We kept him well fed with chicken parts that my mother would provide, and so there was no real reason for him to go out foraging for food in the creek. But it didn't take long before the gator was big enough that you had to have two hands to pick him up, and then when you picked him up and carried him down to the creek, he was quite in his own element. That means he really liked the water and he felt quite at home in that little creek. He would move around on the shore and swim around in the clear water, and just have an enjoyable time. So did we!*

One day we were playing in the creek and the gator headed for the culvert. Once he got into that culvert, we couldn't see him anymore, and we couldn't go after him. While he was small enough to get in there, we were not that small. Once he got in, he did not come back out. He had escaped the prisons of our bathtub, buckets, and creek. He found a new home in the wild. Fred and I didn't know what to do. We went home and got our big brother, Marcus, to come down to the creek and help us find him. We didn't want to tell anybody about it because we thought we might be in trouble, so we just told my mother, and she surmised that that was OK. That gator had gone back into nature as one might expect would be appropriate, but we were missing our gator. We never saw Mister Gator again!

Time went on and several years later, we had another alligator experience. This one was in the town of Ocilla, Georgia, about a 30-minute drive from our home.

My parents had lived in Ocilla for a while before they were married or just after they were married. Ocilla was where my parents' best friends lived, and we spent many, many days and nights over in Ocilla. Marion and Clydie had a couple of ponds over there. He was quite a farmer, and he also owned a feed mill where other farmers would take their corn. As is most often the case with farmers, he also owned some farm animals.

The mill was really cool. They had machines that would take the corn off the cob, and then they would package it in bags or even sell truckloads of corn for other farmers or cattlemen to buy. It was a big industrial operation with big round silos that would hold truckloads of corn.

Marion had two ponds, and we could go over there and fish any time we wanted to. We would catch a lot of fish in those ponds. Sometimes the bass would be a foot long and two or three pounds, and sometimes – most of the time – we would catch bream or white perch, sometimes called sunfish.

These were fish that were smaller, about the size of an adult's hand. We would sometimes catch twenty of them in a day, or even more. We had a wonderful time fishing in that pond.

There were some turtles in that pond too, and they would swim up to the area not too far from your boat. If you were fishing off the land, they would swim up beside you and stick their head up. Occasionally when you'd get a bite on your pole, you'd think you had a fish, but you really didn't. It was just a turtle down there eating your worm. They were sneaky and seemed to be able to make you think you had a fish about to bite your worm only to find the worm was gone from the hook when you pulled it out of the water.

The turtles got to be a problem because there were just too many of them. Marion would put fresh fish from the local fishery in his pond every year. Sometimes a couple of thousand fish were put into the pond. Those fish would grow, but not all of them would live a long life because the turtles would eat them. The pond got very infested with turtles. The turtles would eat those little fish and the turtles got fat. Fishing wasn't so great sometimes, because the turtles had eaten so many of the fish.

Marion was unsure about how to handle his turtle problem. Marion was quite a fisherman, so he would often go to Florida to fish in the Gulf of Mexico.

Someone suggested that he bring back an alligator the next time he went to Florida. In those days, you could buy an alligator, but I never was sure if he was supposed to bring it back to Georgia or not. Regardless, he did purchase the alligator and he did bring it back to Ocilla. Upon his return to Ocilla, he put it in his pond.

Well, initially the gator was very small and didn't have much impact. However, as the gator ate fish and turtles, he grew to about six feet long. As he grew, the turtle population got smaller and smaller.

One funny thing this gator did was bellow. A bellow is a loud noise made by an animal. Other animals bellow too. Cows bellow and so do wild cattle like bison and buffalo, as well as crocodilians, alligators, oxen, bulls, moose, hippopotamus, rhinoceros, and several other animals. And this gator liked to bellow! He would float along the top of the water, glide up to a nearby fisherman, open his mouth wide, and make a loud bellow. It seemed like a yawn of some sort. Then he would close his mouth and swim gently away.

Marion also raised farm animals, and most of them would come down to the corner of the pond to drink water, cool off from the hot South Georgia heat, and then go back into the fields or in the area full of trees and bushes that was near the pond.

Every day or two, Marion would drive through the pasture to the pond and count his animals. There were 26 cows, four goats, four adult pigs with about sixteen piglets – baby pigs. Marion would go out most days and count to make sure all his farm animals were where they were supposed to be. Sometimes a cow might jump the fence and get onto the highway that ran down the side of the pasture. So it was important for farmers to know where their animals were almost every day.

The pigs would have little babies called piglets. And the piglets were little tiny things, about the size of a small dog, but they would grow very fast if fed properly. And so, these pigs would get counted each day, and soon Marion noticed that some of the piglets were missing, but it wasn't the big pigs, it was the little piglets. And as animals in the wild often do, there was a chance the piglet just died because he got sick. But when more than one or two ended up missing, it raised some suspicion.

Marion tried to figure out the cause of his smaller and smaller piglet population. One day he and his wife were out fishing on the pond, and the alligator came up beside them, opened his mouth, and bellowed loudly. It scared Marion's wife, Clydie. She ran off the boat dock into the yard and away from the gator. She didn't care too much for that big old alligator. Marion wasn't so scared of it, because he had been seeing the alligator for a long time. But make no mistake about it, Marion realized how dangerous that gator could be.

Well, that was the day Marion put two and two together and figured out that there was a good chance the gator had gotten so big and so hungry that it might be eating the piglets. After all, most of the turtles had been eaten already. But eating the piglets was not acceptable to most pig farmers, and so Marion had to do something about that. The only real option was to kill the alligator or to try and capture him and move him to some other place. But that was not practical because Marion had no place to move him and the capture of an alligator his size would be very difficult and very dangerous. Marion asked his son to take his rifle, go down to the pond, and kill that gator. Walter shot the gator that day. The ole alligator went under the water and never surfaced again.

Nobody knows what happened to that gator, but no more pigs were missing after that.

Today, many say that it is extremely dangerous to swim in some of the rivers and ponds in South Georgia because many of the rivers and ponds have alligators in them. Just like many of the ponds in Florida have alligators. Who would have thought that the solution to the turtle problem would have ended up being a problem itself?

Mischievous Stories

Chapter Six – That Darn Hammer

It was a yellow trailer that my daddy used to haul cow manure (poop) from my uncle's farm to our backyard. That manure was used to fertilize the tomato plants we planted each year and tied up with string under an old swing set covered with some four-inch chicken wire. The plants we grew each year provided excellent tomatoes for the bacon, lettuce, and tomato sandwiches we had almost daily during tomato season.

South Georgia was a large producer of tomatoes for our nation, and we had a large tomato packaging plant in my hometown. It was great to have it there because they always needed workers, and school kids that wanted to work could go over there almost any time of day and start working. They paid by the hour and didn't care how long you stayed. Normally, the tasks assigned to these types of part-time workers were sorting tomatoes that came down the line into boxes or moving a bunch of boxes from one place to another. I enjoyed working there and particularly enjoyed the paycheck we got every two weeks.

My mother would "can" some of the tomatoes we grew at home for use later in the year. I never understood why it was called canning since the tomatoes ended up in a jar and not a can, but that is the way they defined it. Ladies in the South always canned stuff like jelly, fruit, tomatoes, beans, and most everything that farmers grew.

The manure had to be shoveled from a cow pen into the trailer, and we would make the 55-mile trip from Tifton to Ochlocknee, Georgia, each spring. We did this particular trip solely for the purpose of gathering cow poop. My brother and I would be given a shovel and sent into the cow pen to shovel a trailer full of cow poop. The trailer had a wooden floor and wooden sides and a place to slide wooden boards into each end of the trailer to make a box with no top. We shoveled cow manure until the trailer was full to the top and then some.

Once we made the drive back to Tifton and to our home on Murray Avenue, we would have to unload the trailer into a pile in our backyard. My mother and father would then shovel the correct amount of cow manure into the area where they would soon plant the tomato plants. After that, we would rinse out the trailer and let it dry.

That trailer was also used to haul the wooden boat my dad had built. Together with a small Evinrude motor, a live well for fish in the middle of the boat and three seats from the front to the back of the boat, we had a package that was perfect for the lakes, ponds, and rivers of South Georgia. The live well was filled with water from two holes in the bottom, and when you caught a fish, you would put that fish in the live well where he would swim around while you caught other fish.

When I was about six or seven years old, the trailer happened to be parked alongside 22nd Street on the side of the road that bumped against our backyard. My brother Fred and our neighbor Terry were under the trailer, and for some reason, I had a hammer. I think we had been nailing something we probably should not have been nailing.

As the police car came up the hill from Hall Avenue toward Wilson Avenue, it rolled past Murray Avenue and alongside the yellow trailer under which the three of us were playing.

On a whim and without much thought, I picked up the hammer and decided to throw it over the police car into the pasture on the other side of 22nd Street. I never intended to hit the police car, but in a moment of mischief, the hammer flew through the air towards the police car.

Higher and higher it went as it came from under the yellow trailer. As the police car began to pass us we all heard a terrible sound as the hammer struck the police car behind the back seat of the car near the trunk. That hammer hit right next to the place where you put in the gas.

"Run," said one of the boys, and in a flash we were out from under the boat trailer and running through our backyard and away from the stopped police car.

I think the police were trying to figure out what had happened. They got out of their car and walked back to where the hammer lay on the on the dirt road that was 22nd Street. Fred and Terry ran through our backyard and into our friend Tommy's backyard, and I ran to our back porch and into the house. Fred and Terry were both a year or so older than me, but I knew the error I had made and decided to run into the house and tell my mother.

"I didn't mean to do it," I exclaimed, "but I threw a hammer and it hit a police car and the police got out and are in the street next to our house. What should I do?"

"Go into Marc's room and hide under the bed," instructed my mother. My older brother, Marcus, or Marc for short, had his own room at the end of the house. I went there to hide.

I think my mother thought I was playing a practical joke on her. But by the time the police knocked on our back door, I was shaking like a leaf under the bed in Marc's room.

My mother explained to the police that her six-year-old son had committed that crime and that I had *come inside the house and confessed. She said that I would be appropriately punished. She also advised them that she would gladly pay for any damages that the hammer might have caused to the police car.*

The police were more than understanding and agreed that it was a foolish childhood event and they felt sure my mother would take care of my error in judgment and my bad aim. There was no significant damage to the police car, so my parents did not have to pay for any damages.

I never intended to hit that police car. It was just a mistake for which I was very sorry and for which I hid under the bed until the police were gone. That hammer was supposed to go over the police car, not hit it!

Sometimes we make poor decisions and do not think them through. Throwing the hammer over a police car was not my brightest idea. On top of it being a bad idea, my ability to complete that task was poor as well. I was lying on the ground when I threw the hammer and just did not have the ability to get enough height on that throw to go over the police car.

Good plans are well thought out and done with precision. In other words, they are well executed. The same is true for planning your education, or preparing for a test, or catching fish, or any number of other tasks. You must think about what you want to accomplish and then the steps that you must take to accomplish the task.

To catch a fish, you normally need a pole, some bait, a cork, a sinker, a fish hook, fishing line, a permit to fish, a place to go, a way to get there, and an adult to go with you unless you have a pond in your backyard. All these things must be planned for. But when you don't think about your entire project, you might go off with a pole, some line, a hook, and sinker, and get to the pond with no bait. Fish will not bite a hook that has no bait on it. Without proper planning, your chance of catching a fish would be unlikely.

Remember....

As you go through life, think about the things you want to do, talk it over with your friends or parents or other adults, and then

gather all the things you need

to complete your task successfully.

Good planning and good decisions will make everything come out better.

Mischievous Stories

Chapter Seven – Big Tires

Wouldn't it really suck to die under two huge wheels of an even huger truck? And worse than that, after you just paid to have your car tuned up and in great running condition. Well, that's what almost happened to me in 1983.

Who in their right mind would not want a 1976 Plymouth Duster?   What do you mean, what's that? Even though it was not as classy as the Mustangs of the 1960s and 1970s, it was a good car – reliable, somewhat sporty, two-door, blue in color, and it had a decent engine that was strong enough to give it some spunk, but not too wild. Gas was running about 85 cents per gallon and the mileage was OK but certainly not great. After all, this car was made of thicker metal than today's cars, so it was kinda heavy. It had served me well since the day I picked it up from the Plymouth dealership on Broad Street in Richmond, Virginia, in September of 1975 when I returned from Korea. I had been stationed there as a soldier in 1973.

You see, I was a soldier, and this was my first new car. I joined the United States Army in 1972 after high school graduation, went to basic combat training at Fort Jackson, South Carolina, and then to Fort Lee for supply training. After that, it was off to

Korea, where I was a truck driver, an automotive parts clerk, and then a computer operator. It was a valuable experience for me, and I came back to Fort Lee, Virginia, to teach school in a supply course for new soldiers. I had ordered my blue Plymouth Duster from a car sales place in Seoul, Korea, called the Post Exchange. It was a store mostly for American soldiers. My car was to be delivered to Richmond, where I would pick it up as I returned to America.

Of course, by the time this near-death challenge presented itself, the ol' Duster had been around for several years and broken in by two children, Kelly and Christopher, who were born in 1979 and 1980 to then Sergeant and Mrs. Dave Merritt. From throwing up in their car seats to coloring the inside panels at the age of three and four, you gotta know that this car took a childly beating. But it was our car and we loved it and it was paid for.

As is true with people, when cars start getting a bit older, they require some TLC – tender loving care. This Duster was no different. I had become a bit of a mechanic as I learned to change the brakes and fix what I could on the car when it broke. Fixing your own stuff was a money saver for our family and a necessity. Becoming a pretty good mechanic ran in my wife's family. Her father, Delbert, was an expert.

He could fix anything on a vehicle that was broken, and I learned from him when we took our car to my wife's home in Waynesboro, Virginia. Her brother, Phillip, grew into a skilled technical guy too and he served in the US Army as well.

And then there was James. He was a big man who had served his country well in the army and settled in at a military base near Petersburg, Virginia, called Fort Lee. James managed the Auto Craft Shop, an operation on Fort Lee. James, actually Ryan James but everyone called him James, helped soldiers learn to work on their cars. Fort Lee gave soldiers a place to do the work. It was great. The Auto Craft Shop was complete with several auto lifts on which you could raise your car and work on the stuff under the car without killing your neck and back. James helped me so many times and I learned the ins and outs of fixing my car myself.

So, between Delbert and James, I had two of the finest automotive experts any novice auto repair person could ever want. They both became my friends for life.

Now, I could fix a lot of things, but one that I struggled with was the carburetor. It was a thing on old cars that have been replaced by today's fuel injection and electronic systems that are so precise that it's difficult for a shade-tree-mechanic to work on them. Shade-tree-mechanic is a term that describes people like me who can fix the simpler things on a car. As cars have become more electronically technical, we shade-tree-mechanics have lost the ability to fix many of the components.

So, when my carburetor started to die – or at least got very sick – I had to carry it to someone who had the technology to tune it well. For me, it was a shop in Petersburg, Virginia, that had all the right tools and specialized in tuning up cars like mine for shade-tree-mechanics like me. Who would have ever thought that my life would be almost taken because of the place I chose to have my car repaired…? Or was it my failure to pay attention to the important things that nearly caused my death?

That's why caution and focus are so important. Paying attention to what matters is vital to success in life.

That Duster had taken us from Fort Lee, Virginia, to Fort Benning, Georgia, where I attended Officer Candidate School and received a commission as a Second Lieutenant in the United States Army. From there, it was back to Fort Lee for officer-relevant supply and logistics training. Toward the end of that training, my wife had our first child, Kelly. Soon after that, we were off to Fort Campbell, Kentucky, and into the 101st Airborne Division. I served there for three years, and we had our second child, Christopher. When my three years were up at

Fort Campbell, we returned to Fort Lee for more training. After the training course, I was assigned to Fort Lee for a three-year tour of duty.

 The Duster had been in the shop near the intersection of Interstate 95 and Washington Street in Petersburg for a couple of days as the shop worked on it or as I just waited for my turn in line. The staff at this auto shop were very good and they had all the right tools to do the carburetor job. When they called and said it was ready, I was excited to get it back and had pretty good confidence that it was going to run better.

 Before they worked on the car, it was running rough. It stuttered, sputtered, and stalled. The carburetor that mixed the air and the gas before it entered the engine and exploded was a very important part of the car. These guys fixed it so well. When I cranked the car, I could immediately tell that the job had been done to perfection. The car ran smoothly and there was no more sputtering and stalling. I was good to go.

 And go I did.

 I was so excited about how it was running that I headed out of the parking lot onto Washington Street and almost lost my life. You see, Washington Street is one-way. All the cars go in the same direction. It's not like two-way traffic. I only went one way, but it *was the wrong way…. The good news was that I didn't go very far. In fact, I didn't even get all four tires onto Washington Street before I met a huge dump truck with huge tires.*

There are varied sizes of dump trucks with even larger size tires. And when they are loaded, even when they are not loaded, they are heavy. Dump trucks are some of the toughest trucks in the trucking industry, and they haul all kinds of things around. Sometimes rock, sometimes mulch, sometimes sand, stones, or dirt. You never know, but they can carry a heavy load of cargo and so they must have these huge tires.

The tires on this truck were big! And they were wide too, and because of all the weight, there were two sets of two on the rear of the truck on both sides.

As I drove out the wrong way on the one-way street, I drove under the dump truck that was rolling down the street. The initial crash was a shock and it was over in about three seconds. Then there was a screeching noise as the dump truck driver slammed on his brakes and brought that monster truck to a stop. In the three seconds my car actually touched the dump truck, he rolled over the hood of my car from about the middle of the car to a spot just behind the front wheel. The noise he made was like the crushing of a Coke can as you stomp on it with your foot. And then it was over.

Had I entered that highway three or four seconds sooner, I would have hit the dump truck head on and he would have smashed all my car and not just one corner of the engine hood. He was probably not speeding, but he was loaded, and I watched frantically as those huge tires rolled over the front of my recently repaired Plymouth Duster. Had I been a second or two earlier, I would have hit a huge gas tank that was just behind the driver's door and before you get to the first set of back tires. This might have caused a fire as well as a smashed car.

I was shocked. But I was also quickly impressed with the fact that my life had been spared. I could have easily been dead. Three seconds earlier and I would have been in front of that huge truck, a second or two earlier and I would have hit his huge gas tank and then been crushed by the back tires. No, if I was to hit that truck, I entered the road and struck the truck at just the right place and time and at just the right angle. Because of that, I lived through the accident and didn't even have an injury – not a scratch.

The police came to the scene and made a report. The driver of the dump truck just wanted to go back to work, and his dump truck was no worse for the accident. His tires were not even hurt. He had no dents. The accident was not his fault. He just wanted to go, and the police officer sent him on his way quickly. I had to wait for the tow truck to haul my car away to a repair facility.

My beautiful blue Plymouth Duster was dead, but I lived on. Life is good, but the car that saw the birth of our two children and traveled with us safely through multiple states for about six years was destined for the junkyard. It was now time to buy a new car, and we did. But I declared a new rule for my three- and four-year-old children: NO CRAYONS in the back of our new car! The new rule for me: don't pull out in front of any more dump trucks!

You never know why things happen the way they do. Was I left on this earth for a reason? Was I here to help others as I grew older and served in more important positions in the army and in business? Or was it just chance that death had nearly visited me several times? None of these thoughts escaped my mind.

I still wonder, as I suspect many others do, why am I here and what is my purpose?

How can I help someone today?

Afterword

While the last story in this book is not really "Mischievous" in nature, it was a near-death story. As I mentioned in the preface to this book, we don't know why we are here or if we have a specific purpose for being. In my life, I have taken note that I am fortunate to have survived multiple near-death experiences. I thought it was a good idea to assemble a few of these near-death experiences and share them with some lessons learned and so did my grandchildren.

All my near-death experiences were the result of bad judgment or bad decisions that put me in harm's way. Each could have been avoided if I had thought more about being cautious and if I had not thrown caution to the wind.

Death is not the only reward for foolishness. In any of these situations, my life could have been changed for the worse due to a loss of limb, sight, or any number of other consequences. As you walk through life, think often and well about the consequences of your actions. Consider risk and rewards. Make sound decisions that are not the influence of inappropriate peer pressure or greed.

Live long, live happily, and remember to thank those who help you succeed in your life.

Great Gifts
Mischievous Stories & Soldier Stories (Volume I)

Soldier Stories is a great book for the 16+ age group that's clean, funny, surprising, and focuses on making career impacting decisions and some important lessons in leadership, dignity and respect, mentorship, career management, and ethics.

Soldier Stories is a particularly great gift if you have a Soldier in your family or in your circle of friends. This book has hugely valuable lessons learned over ¼ century of service to America by one Soldier….

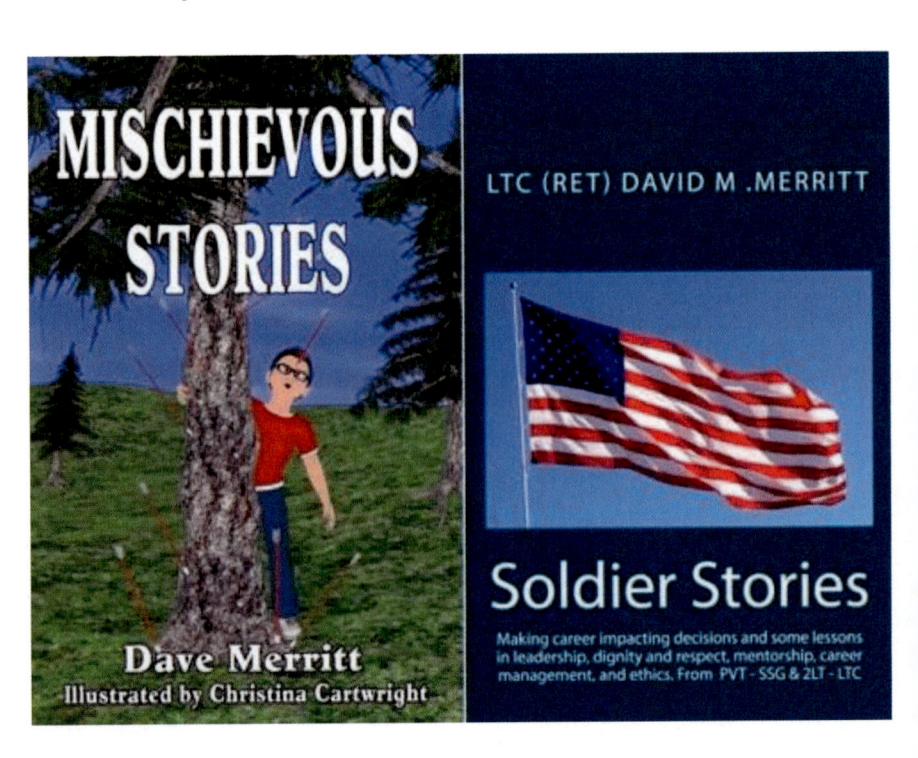

Made in the
USA
Middletown, DE